THE REAPER

BY JOSEPH MCGEE

SNUFF BOOKS
PHILADELPHIA, PA.
SNUFFBOOKS.COM

To you, Reader; the only person I should dedicate this particular story to. For your patience; for your never-ending support. Thank you for the support!

First and foremost, this book would not have been resurrected without the vision of Adam Huber and Snuff Books, for that, they have my utmost gratitude.

For the unending efforts of Eric Enck; for his friendship; for his wise guidance.

This brings me to Joe McKinney: A hell of a writer; a good friend with a lot of advice still up his sleeve—thank you.

To Shaun Jeffrey for his help in sprucing things up and writing the beginning to this book.

CONTENTS

Introduction
By Shaun Jeffrey

The Reaper is an iconic figure that has appeared in most forms of popular culture. In Ingmar Bergman's film, *The Seventh Seal*, a medieval knight returning from a crusade plays a game of chess with Death, with the knight's life depending upon the outcome of the game. In 1991's *Bill and Ted's Bogus Journey*, the Grim Reaper is portrayed as a hilarious, unsportsmanlike, mildly sarcastic man who wears a black robe, has white skin, no hair and carries a scythe.

In virtually every countries mythology and religion, Death appears in various guises. In English tales, he is often called the Grim Reaper, and is portrayed as a skeletal figure wearing a black cloak with a hood, his face a mere shadow beneath the cloth. In Hindu scriptures the lord of death is called Yama, or Yamaraj (literally *"the lord of death"*). Yamaraj rides a black buffalo and carries a rope lasso to carry the soul back to his abode called *"Yamalok"*. Lithuanians named Death *Giltinė*, deriving from the word "gelti" (to sting). He even appears in the Bible, Revelation 6:8 - And I looked, and behold a pale horse:

and his name that sat on him was Death, and Hell followed with him.

In fiction, he appears most famously in Book V of *Paradise Lost* by John Milton, where Death, along with Sin, holds the keys to the locked Gates of Hell, and in Terry Pratchett's *Discworld* novels, where he has a walk-on part in every Discworld book; if anyone dies, Death is there to collect them.

But whether serious in nature or used more for comedic effect, at his black heart, the Reaper's purpose never changes: harvester of souls; shepherd of the dead.

But what if the Reaper wants more than that? What if gathering souls isn't enough? What if the Reaper wants to take matters into his own hands? Now up and coming author, Joseph McGee has absorbed these tales from popular culture, twisting them within his mind to conjure up a story that confronts this question, taking the Reaper to a new, bloody extreme.

In musical terms, Blue Oyster Cult sang, (Don't fear) The Reaper.

They had obviously never read McGee's hard-hitting story.

Come on baby (fear the reaper)

Now turn the page, immerse yourself in McGee's world and hope and pray that the shadows you see from the corners of your eyes are just that, because this time, the Reaper is here to kick ass.

Shaun Jeffrey

August 2008

THE REAPER:
THE BEGINNING

Shortly before Maggie's murder:

Dear David,

I'm writing this e-mail because I think something bad may happen to me soon. I stumbled upon something I shouldn't have a long time ago, and now I think it's after me. I might have disturbed it or something, someway… I don't know.

I love you. Please know that. If anything happens to me, please do not go to the old hospital—I'm sure that's where they'll find my car and my body.

It's dangerous there, and I think that's where it resides – somewhere on the sixth floor. Do not come here. Do not go looking for me. Please!

Promise me this – one last thing I ask, make this promise to me.

I love you David.

Maggie

The Reaper

INVITATION

1

The promise of winter's first snowfall whispered in the wind amidst the evening sky. The December wind was chilly and uncommonly cold. The season had dipped quite low in temperature in the past, but this year seemed even colder than those before it.

Maggie had secrets that she hadn't shared since she was a teenager. Secrets that haunted her from a past of misery she tried so hard to forget; recurring, taunting in the back of her mind like a vile memory. Only there was *nothing* fond about that memory. It was horrible and she'd been trying to escape it ever since; changing her name, relocating after her brother and sister died mysteriously within weeks of one another... The torment never stopped in her mind. Neither did the visions she saw every time she closed her eyes. Maggie always knew she wouldn't be set free easily. It would still come after her. Years had passed and *it* was still coming for her, relentless in its pursuit.

The second floor of the old psychiatric facility was used for storage and some executive personnel, downstairs was where management countered the billing process for the affiliated hospitals in the city. None of the current staff that worked there could recall an *incident* in the years they had been there, and not one of them knew the tale. Not one of the fourteen employees working Monday through Friday, nine to five, had heard any of the campfire tales, and a good percentage of them wouldn't believe in such ridiculous notions anyway. Not too many people did anymore, not even those who were religious and believed in a higher power. No one would ever look at the evil point of view, but where there is good, there is always evil. They go hand-in-hand, like the sun and the moon. One will rise, the other will fall. A decade later, it was replaying the memory of the sixth floor, as if the hospital had its own life force hard at work, an attempt to claim more patients.

Rumor had it – as Maggie had read on websites and yellowed newspapers in the bowels of the country library – that a clinically insane young woman took the lives of eighteen staff members in the hospital after she'd seen the child with black eyes. It was a brutal slaying, the killing far from the worst part – that's not why it was believed haunted ground. It was the manner in which she did it. A form of torture to some, as if they wanted to give up information to stop her, but they just didn't know what to say.

People said you could still hear the screams of the innocent victims begging for their lives. Handprints of blood had shown up on the walls; the sound of shattering glass where an orderly was thrown from the window still reiterated on the darkest of nights.

On the night she turned nineteen Maggie met David. He was finishing up an assignment from Boston University, an independent study of human behavior on the street for his psychology class. He was jotting down notes in his spiral notebook when he had bumped into her, stirring up an angry mutter of "watch where you're going." They stood beneath the canopy of the irregularly positioned spruce branches, watching them wave in the wind, oblivious to everything except each other. And that was when David asked if he could buy her a cup of coffee. She smiled and agreed. Down the strip on Lakeview was a little coffee shop with drinks and pastries. They talked for almost an hour, until the passing showers swept away the spring afternoon.

David was well-rounded. He had the looks and a great personality that Maggie adored. He had an endearing *I'm-no-better-than-anyone* attitude. He was a writer, and his latest novel was being optioned for film. He was making it in the world, one word at a time.

Maggie worked as a regional manager for a chain of pet stores, which required her to visit every store on her list once a week or so to make sure things were going as smoothly as could be expected. That was her job – and those sixty hours a week were a killer – calling for takeout and a movie on Friday nights to ease the stress of exhausting days.

They moved into an apartment together after their first year of dating. It was more of a test than a living arrangement. If they could pull this off for a little while then perhaps wedding bells would be the next step. But it never got that far. It lasted another couple of years, until the fighting, the constant bickering and the secrecy became too much for both of them to handle, especially David.

Then there was her secret obsession, which had made David believe, at first, that she was hiding some sick sexual fetish. Maybe she enjoyed the hardcore stuff; perhaps she liked the ladies, too. For all he knew, she could've been wanted by the FBI for murder. He never asked about it, of course. He didn't ask her anything, and maybe that had been the problem to begin with.

But he found her secret far worse than a kinky thrill ride or an arrest warrant.

Playing with the dead seemed irresponsible and somewhat sadistic, even to Maggie. She knew she hadn't the right to be playing god in her games of the occult. She'd read too many books, seen too many movies – it never worked out in the end. It was just tomfoolery at work. She was looking for excitement at any cost, for that something other than Nowheresville to visit. She wanted to be scared. It's like teenagers wanting to see the goriest horror movie just to feel their heart jump from their chest, their breath stolen in suspense.

She found it in the black eyes of the child on the sixth floor with the help of a local man from Braintree. He had written *Can't Find Heaven or Hell*, a book barely two-hundred pages long, which spoke of ten different locations in the Massachusetts area where kindred spirits lingered as a result of brutal attacks. Some stories dated back hundreds of years, while some were just a decade old – like the hospital. She had promised herself she would visit all the sites that the author, Michael Alexander spoke of.

If no one had witnessed this back then, then how could you find absolute truth?

And that's when her obsession with the old psychiatric hospital progressed. *Obsession* might've been too loose of a word – it was a damn addiction if there ever was one. Like nicotine, she just couldn't get enough of the elusive mystery. To her, the hospital came to life. It lived, breathed and still listened to every single assonance that played in its halls; all of the cries, the tears, every grumble of pain, and absence of spirit. It always listened.

The author of the book wrote the most grotesque sequences she had read outside of a Clive Barker novel. But the worst part was that they were *true*. The author claimed to have gotten his information from old newspaper articles, police reports, and living witnesses. Not one word of his stories was fabricated, he claimed in an interview with the *Boston Herald*.

The hospital was not the most grotesque story in there, although it was close. Maggie considered the story titled *Hell's Horseman* the pinnacle of heinous acts. She didn't dare think of that story again, and would never again return to Old Mill Road in Ware. *Oh God, never!* Not if what the author said was true. That was the only location in the novel in which she felt she would break her promise.

She wanted to feel alive, and somehow that meant making friends with the dead. She thought, deep in her subconscious, that it would somehow make up for the lack of friends she had growing up. Being in an abusive family for so long did not warmly invite friends to come over and play. She was adopted shortly after the Department of Social Services had found out about her rough dealings – that her mother was using cocaine and her father drank and bucked his hips at every whore he could find after cashing in his dismal weekly paycheck. The constant bruises on her legs and back and face were clear evidence she needed out of the home. She was seven when she went to live with some nice folks who owned a farm just outside of town.

In the wake of the night, she found herself staring up and down at the tall building. The door was closed and locked by now. The traffic on the street was sparse and no one would think twice that a young, decently-groomed woman could possibly be a burglar.

Regardless of the potential repercussions of her plot, she felt a special invitation.

And they were waiting for her on the sixth floor.

REPRESENTING DEATH

2

The elevator sprung open with clinks and clanks from the hidden machinery inside the shaft. It was an older model that had been installed in the eighties, and it had no advanced settings simply to reach the operating floors of one and two. It wasn't sophisticated and there wasn't a large budget to upgrade the elevators to a more contemporary style. It was called from the sixth floor – and on occasion it went up and down by itself. The employees just thought it was a malfunction or an electrical short.

The staff was reluctant to take it upstairs, and so they used the stairs on the opposite side of the building near Elevator B, most with ease, except for Billy Wingham, a large, older man in his fifties who tipped the scale at over three-hundred pounds. He usually sent one of the others up for him; he didn't want to have a heart attack from climbing a set of fourteen steps. He'd be embarrassed, even in his grave.

Maggie brushed the blonde curls from the front of her glasses as she used a tool kit to break the lock and allow herself access. Into the elevator she went, and looked up at the ceiling as if she expected a pair of eyes to be watching her every move or to find a warning sign from a friendly spirit ordering her off the elevator – and damn quick! She would've followed those instructions and never looked back.

Without pressing the button identified with a bold *6* in the center of it, the elevator doors shut and it began to move.

She counted the highlighted numbers in the center above the doors in a whisper. "Two... Three... Four... Five... Six..."

She carefully looked out at the darkened floor when the doors banged into the walls. The only light came through the windows from the streets; passing cars, street lamps, businesses not quite yet closed...

...and that was when she saw the child with the oozing black eyes. So dark they were barely recognizable, murky as infinite space, lurking through the rooms with the same laughter found on a playground, on slides and swings and sandboxes. Like a phantom, he faded in and out of sight.

He represents death she thought.

Legends of the children with black eyes went a long way back, as far back as the fifteenth century, she knew. They were accused kidnappers and murderers, but most of all, scare artists, and no one knew quite what they were or where they had come from. It was just another paranormal mystery shoved into a paper tray at Maggie's computer desk.

It was close and personal.

The woman patient had stabbed most of them, spraying blood on the floors and walls, and then she found enough strength to throw someone through the window. Another she electrocuted, using an emergency defibrillator on the highest voltage setting, literally cooking the man's skin, leaving it extra crispy, as echoes of screams surged through the building like an incoming tide. She gutted one nurse with a ballpoint pen, and used the small puncture to rip her hand into the stomach and pull out whatever she could grab onto, and then she splayed the nurse's head with a surgical tool. Before she could get to victim nineteen, one of the orderlies, with his last breath, shoved a two-CC syringe through her left eye, piercing her retina and forcing its way to her brain. The man fell to the floor, blood pouring out of his chest and dribbling down the corners of his mouth, knowing that he had saved at least one person. And then he knew no more.

The woman had died almost instantly. She'd fallen to the floor silently. Blood pooled out of her head and trickled onto the oyster grey tile, the syringe still firmly wedged in her eye socket.

When the police arrived on scene, they had called it one of the worst mass murders in the history of Massachusetts, and the local papers had splashed that quote across their headlines for weeks.

That was ten years ago.

Walking through the dark halls, Maggie heard whispering so soft and gentle that she strained to make out complete words.

Something stood behind her.

She let out a cry, but no one could hear her. She backpedaled to the windows, to be closer to the ebbing light, before full darkness came.

The windows were grungy, thick with dust and cobwebs. She brushed them away with the sleeve of her shirt, hoping more light would come in, hoping that she could lift the window up and yell down for help, for someone to call the police! But the window wouldn't budge.

She had never been scared like this before.

Whispers wrestled around her.

Something seemed to brush up her legs.

Something was *there*.

Now, she was on the run from something she didn't understand. Something she should've stayed clear from. He called himself *The Reaper, father of the black-eyed children.*

And He was coming.

The Reaper

THE END IS NEAR

3

Maggie shimmied her way over to a thin brown carpet in one of the offices. She felt a chill rush through her. The door clicked shut. The windows, like the ones by the nurses' station, were locked tightly.

Something else was in here with her. She could sense it.

She turned and saw the child again, staring at her with a tilted head, as if confused by her appearance.

I shouldn't be here.

She panicked. She felt her heart race as she collapsed to the ground, banging her head off the only piece of furniture in the room, a desk centered on nothing.

Shortly after losing consciousness, her eyes blinked open. Her vision pooled back to normalcy, and she found herself bound with leather wrist and ankle straps on a vacant hospital bed. Before she could determine this world was so much different than the one she knew just a short while ago, *He* stood over her.

He was the one she knew of. *He* was the one that resided here on the sixth floor. She read about beings like this, but not one scripture or literary piece ever described what He would look like.

The Reaper, an apparition that seemed much more real than a translucent body, was draped in dark clothing and walked weightlessly. He watched over her, waiting for her to awaken to a full state of awareness. His tawny figure walked to the counter in the back of the small hospital room, which featured chipped yellow paint and a small window only a cat might fit through. The door was a solid white with a square window for onlookers to peer through, at a patient undergoing tests that were most likely neither ethical, nor legal.

He examined surgical supplies of all shapes and sizes, and brought them over to her wordlessly. Could He say a word at all? Maggie wasn't even sure if breathing was part of his character. He was taut, emotionless, his face concealed by a draping cloth, covering his nose and mouth.

Maggie was scared but more curious than anything. *Who is he? What is he? Where did he come from?* Those and other questions tangled at her psyche.

He looked at her – or at least that's what she thought it was, considering she couldn't see any eyes in the enveloping darkness.

He never spoke. Not once. It sent a message to Maggie that she was perhaps going mad. That's how she knew it was called *The Reaper*, at last.

He was what had probed her to come here.

He took the metallic instruments, looked her over once again, and dug under her skin, fast and mean with a ridged scalpel aged a decade or more. It probed into her skull and Maggie heard the metal scraping its way into her.

Fear overcame her. She screamed in agony as her blood splashed against the walls in a clean ruptured spray. It dribbled down the corners of her mouth as the blade searched deeper. Her eyes were wide and glaring. Another slice, and another. Performing a poor-man's-surgery. A deep incision, under and past her scalp. She heard a loud cracking sound and wondered what was to become of her. She felt lukewarm – and tired. And then she went into a deep sleep, with tears streaming down her now lifeless face, culminating in a river of suffering.

It was the next morning before the police found Maggie's corpse lying lifeless on the table in Room 604, after a worker reported a break in. A thorough search of the facility had revealed Maggie's body, soaked from head-to-toe in her own blood.

"The investigation is ongoing with no leads to signify a single or multiple suspects in this case," the police sergeant had reported to a news crew parked out front.

But *The Reaper* was out there.

And Maggie now wandered the halls of the sixth floor.

TO SURVIVE

4

Survival is a tricky thing, David Bells thought solemnly. *But Maggie's a survivor. She'll make it,* he assured himself to whatever nonsense this message encoded.

An unsuspected rain fell outside without warning. No thunder preceded the cascade, no wind came howling in. It was as surreal as a horrible nightmare could ever become.

David held on to the printed version of the e-mail from Maggie. He was not an officer of the law and did not have any special training, though sometimes he did research on it for his stories… But that didn't compare to the real training, the real exercises, the real fear – none of it.

Earlier that night, David was restless in his bed. He was trying hard to fall asleep, but couldn't quite reach that point. He blamed part of the problem on the streaming blue glow of the alarm clock in the back corner of his room. Since he was awake and had nowhere to be the next day, he thought he'd write something that night, or finish editing his new novel and maybe get it to the publisher a month early. But first, he instinctually checked his e-mail and found the message from Maggie.

Sitting at his desk, holding the paper in his hand, on the verge of sobbing in fret, he turned his imagination loose like a perilous dream embarking on his nights. That night would be one of uncertain expectations and indecisive amounts of stress, like a plague of syphilis. He did not know the true meaning of the letter, or if Maggie really was in danger. Maybe it was just a tired attempt to mend things between them, for him to race off in the middle of the night and be her savior. To rescue her from whatever demons awaited. But she had never been one to be reduced to such dramatic measures, to suggest that her life were somehow in danger from some *thing*.

Or was *it a cry for help?*

Would she hurt *herself?*

In the kitchen of his newly purchased house, he slouched on the bench by the kitchen table centered in the middle of the room.

The rain pounded against the pane of the window, as lightning flickered through the sky of the unexpected December storm. And by the light of the submerged moon, he sat and wondered.

This can't be a good sign he told himself.

23

The only solution, he thought, was to head over to Maggie's place and find out exactly what the e-mail was all about.

Shadows surged through the kitchen, catching his attention. They taunted him, cornering him with their darkness. But there was no one in his home. No visible person, and yet, man-shaped silhouettes filled the room.

As the sounds of thunder ricocheted through the air, the windows in his home exploded in shards of glass.

The shadows gathered around him, circling him, waiting.

He wasn't alone anymore.

The Reaper

SHADOWS

5

The movement of shadows quickened frantically, like an epilepsy victim flailing about his hands. David leapt to his feet, wearing only a v-neck t-shirt and silk pajama bottoms, and ran back to his bedroom. He considered calling 911, and then he assessed the situation.

They're shadows. Something caused by the lightning or the traffic outside, he calmed himself. But even he didn't believe it. Nor could he believe that he was being contacted by otherworldly beings in the form of shadows. That was just nonsense. *Utter nonsense.*

This was something he could add to one of his books, perhaps. *This is not real life*, he thought to himself. *No fucking way!*

David quickly threw off his clothes and put on dungarees, adding a hooded sweatshirt over his plain white shirt. He slid on his sneakers, not pausing for socks, and was ready to bolt from his home, should the situation require it. He was more concerned with *how* he'd be getting out of the house, if he had to, in a hurry.

He shoved his wallet and keys deep into his pockets. Surreal moans and hollers echoed down the hall, reminding him of the classic *A Christmas Carol,* with Scrooge's former business partner Marley rattling his chains.

Something was out there. No mistaking that – but what?

Confusion was settling in now. He had only one way to leave. David felt the imminent danger lurking through his kitchen and glanced out the front door, weighing his options; beyond stood a hall and a flight of stairs, with access to a window. It was a second floor drop. He might break a bone, he considered, but he surely wouldn't die –not from just a second story fall.

He knew he was running out of options.

The screams were getting louder.

Closer.

Fear had frozen him. Tears were rolling down his face uncontrollably. He was terrified, more terrified than any of the characters he created in his stories.

What the hell was in that e-mail?

The hell if he knew. Dead souls were rushing toward him. He could feel it, sense them coming… coming for him.

My name is Legion, for we are many.

That same verse repeated in his head, but these were not his own thoughts.

The Reaper will come to play. The Reaper will come to play. For all of you, stay out of his way. The Reaper will come to play.

He held his hands to his ears, trying to block out the sound, but it was no use. It was coming from *inside* him. He screamed, cried for it to stop, until he got down on his knees and prayed to God. And for a brief moment it did stop. It allowed him a short moment of tranquility and soundlessness. But it began again; a song playing in his head, one that he'd never heard before, a melody that could only come from a horror movie.

The Reaper will come to play. The Reaper will come to play. For all of you, stay out of his way. The Reaper will come to play. And we know how to play the game, the rest he will maim. The Reaper will come to play.

The sickening riddle in his head played over and over again, relentlessly tugging at his sanity. David opened the window and kicked out the screen. One leg went over the edge, his hands gripped tight to the sill. The other leg slipped over, and he found the strength to lower his hundred ninety pound body down a few feet before letting go and crashing to the front yard. The soft dirt and grass broke the brunt of his fall, but a sharp pain rose in his left leg, like it had been slugged with a blunt object.

David raced to his car, dragging along his hurt limb, and fumbled for his keys. He opened the driver side door and slid in, locking the doors and pausing to catch his breath. He took a few seconds to collect himself and nurse his throbbing leg, cradling it in his hands.

The shadows swam on the Earth like shades of seagulls flying high above, waiting for an old man to toss out moldy bread for lunch. They rushed to him, racing in a full panic.

He shoved the key in the ignition of his '05 BMW and threw it into drive, squealing out of his driveway, burning rubber on the asphalt as he headed to Maggie's house.

SAVING GRACE

6

David drove to the countryside. That was where Maggie lived with her family. It was a good forty-five minutes to get out there, but worth every minute if it meant he could save Maggie from a less than pleasant fate, like the one he'd just endured.

The ground was wet. A hard rain came down, the harsh drops raping the sodden stretch of highway he traveled. David kept the speed at sixty, and when traffic dissipated, he floored the gas pedal, cranking it to eighty to shave off a precious few minutes.

His mind swam with the horrible possibilities of what could have happened to Maggie. There was more of a story than she had put in the message; that much was obvious. A hole in her column of truth. There was something more. And David knew it was impossible for him to guess what, exactly, was waiting for him at Maggie's house. Would it be more shadows flailing in the night? Or something far worse than that?

What the hell is going on!?

He'd rather think that nothing was the matter. Everyone was fine and nothing, absolutely nothing, was out of the ordinary. But what was that song in his head? It sounded like a choir of children like in those *Nightmare on Elm Street* movies. Something was terribly wrong, beyond his own comprehension. He couldn't understand the singing in his head, or what it meant. Who was *The Reaper?*

The answer was as obvious as it was smart: someone he didn't want to piss off. At least not more than he somehow had already.

He thought about slowing down, pulling into a gas station on the highway, and turning right around. This was too much for him to handle—too much for most people to handle. This was past the realm of surreal, and on to a blown-out nightmare coming to life.

His heart raced inside of him like a jackhammer. Anxiety tightened his chest and he tried to let out calming breaths of air as he gently released the gas pedal, slowing down. He pulled over, stopped in the breakdown lane, and shifted the gears into park, pressing the button for his emergency lights.

It took a few minutes for him to calm his nerves, to relax before he could try it again.

"What the fuck is happening to me?" he said aloud, lashing out and pounding the roof with both fists.

"What the hell is going on?"

But he knew his query was not one that could be easily answered.

After a systematic deep breath, he shifted back into gear and pulled away from the shoulder.

David pictured the last night he and Maggie had shared together. They hadn't had sex – opting instead for what most people would call "the talk." It was the conversation in which they found out about all of the previously hidden details of their pasts and their ambitions for the future. He kept replaying the conversation about before Maggie was adopted. How she was abused, both physically and mentally. There'd been some debate as to which had caused the most damage. But for David, the strain of dealing with mental abuse when one was a mere child would take its toll for years. Or at least that's what he'd heard on one of those daytime talk shows.

The remainder of the drive was slow and uneventful. No travelers seemed to be steering their way through a place that David normally called the "boonies."

Maggie's house was in the middle of nowhere; the nearest neighbor owned a ranch half a mile up the road. Her family had lived in the same location for four generations. David and Maggie had even discussed moving in there someday; raising a family, living the American Dream. It had been normal for them. They had been crazy for each other, though David seldom admitted it to her *or* himself. He knew how he felt inside – and fuck, now he hoped it wasn't too late to tell her himself.

No lights were on in the house. No porch light washing a soft, welcoming yellow glow over the chipped floorboards, as it normally did. No flickering beams of the television inside. Nothing but the secluded darkness, trapped within the confines of the house. In the daylight, you could see its red exterior and the stable a couple of hundred yards out back where horses could have been kept, although they haven't had livestock in the family for a few decades.

David turned off the ignition, stepped out of the car, and walked up the front steps, careful to stay in the beacons of the headlights he'd left on. He knocked on the door, gentle at first, then harder as what seemed like minutes went by without a response. The shed to the right of the house, underneath the big oak tree, was where her family normally stowed their vehicles, but it was hard to see a few yards, let alone fifty feet in the pitch black.

He jiggled the handle on the door. It opened. Floorboards beneath him creaked in protesting opposition. The house had been cut off from its electricity; the microwave on the counter gave that much away when he saw its digital clock numbers dark and vacant.

His heart pounded in his chest. It was all he could hear: the thumping of his own heart, the thickness in his own breath.

Maggie.

He walked into the kitchen, which sat adjacent to the front door. No sign of life at all. He crept through each room of the downstairs, finding nothing, and began to make his way upstairs. But first, underneath the kitchen sink, he grabbed the flashlight they had always kept in case of a power failure; something to make the darkness retract, if even for a moment.

He carefully headed up the stairs, shining the light with his arm extended, as if the light were a shield that would protect him. But it wasn't. He knew that.

Something was wrong there.

The upstairs was as quiet and empty as the first floor had been. Dead. Eerily silent. There wasn't a soul in sight.

Then he opened the bedroom door.

They were dead. Mutilated. Her father was decapitated. Her mother was sliced open like a roasted pig. Blood had soaked the sheets of their bed, creating puddles of mortality on the floor.

And suddenly, more shadows came. They thrashed like a possessed preacher speaking the End Times from the Holy Scriptures, waving like palm trees in a tropical storm

THE REAPER IS COMING

7

The house had become an evil place, a stark contrast to the peaceful country residence he had once known. It was now a forbidden, mocking chamber of dissolution. Dead bodies lay in the bedroom, resting in a forever-sleep.

David backed against the wall in disbelief, cornering himself in, and realizing that *something* was doing this. *Something* had killed them, though he did not know *who* or *what*. Just *something*. A mass murderer. Some sick Satanist running loose. The shadows. It was up for the detectives to decide, but he wouldn't risk calling the cops, not while he was still there. It would raise a lot of questions and tie him up for hours at the police station, where he'd be interrogated for answers he couldn't possibly give.

The Reaper is coming.

The same voice echoed in his head like personal demons, taunting him to solve the riddle.

He left the house, but before he did so, he made sure to wipe off the doorknob. He didn't want any fingerprints to be traced back to him. And like cops sometimes do, they'd hold him on it for a day at least, though he'd done nothing wrong.

He would be the only suspect, until some motive, another suspect, another jilted lover could be found to justify the evil deed. That was something he wasn't going to risk. Not until he found Maggie.

Maggie.

God, where is she?

He looked at the sky. The rain had disappeared; blustery blocks of black-grey clouds rolled overhead and gave the promise of another storm, for another time.

He climbed into his car and sat idling. Across the street, he stared at a small broken-down shed. A blockade of flowerpots encircled it – a hobo's retreat. Something strong enough to block the wind, solid enough to keep dry.

And the waiting began.

He thought and thought.

The crescent moon broke through the low sky.

And suddenly he remembered. He knew where she was.

Maggie's obsession – she loved old hospitals. David remembered her reading some book on a local nut-house around these parts. That's where she had to be. For some unexplained reason, that's where she *had* to be. He knew it. It came to him like a long forgotten childhood memory.

Joseph McGee

She was there.

The Reaper

IN THE WAKE OF THE MORNING

8

At first David scoured the roads, searching for her body. He examined the passing farms as he traveled, trying her cell phone countless times, but it always went straight to voicemail. Dawn would be coming soon. Morning would break loose on this town before he had a chance to resolve anything. He felt useless. For the first time in his life, he felt like he wasn't worth *jack shit*.

He heard movement in the woods.

It was just the critters that preferred to sneak out after nightfall, cloaked by the darkness, invisible to see.

Maggie *needed* him, and so he picked up speed. There was no way of telling if a body had been dropped off in the woodlands. He would barely be able to tell if one would be lying just off the road in a ditch, exhumed by the ricochet of his high-beams.

A woman like Maggie has many needs, David thought. But the main need right then was to be *rescued*. Some kind of bad bullshit was going down.

His mind reverberated back to the old campfire stories.

They came to him like a revelation.

The old hospital.

A sense of rage shot over him and it was about to drive *him* to murder. He would *kill* whoever it was that brutally slaughtered Maggie's parents.

Oh, dear God, what if the same thing happened to her? What if she's dead just like them and I can't find her?

He reached for the cell phone to call for the police, but he had a better idea – something that would not link him to being at their house, frantic and worried in the middle of the night.

He drove back to the house, and headed inside with the borrowed flashlight in hand.

In the kitchen, he grabbed four or five sheets from the paper towel roll and picked up the phone hanging on the wall. There was a dial tone. He dialed 911 and waited for the operator to pick up. Just as someone did, he let the phone fall to the floor, making an echoing sound on the other end: a sure sound of distress. The police would be there momentarily, and David knew that he'd better high tail it out of there, and quickly. He couldn't possibly begin to explain what had happened. He couldn't begin to understand why some sick *sonofabitch* would murder such sweet people like Maggie's folks. They had liked David since day one. They even called him

Maggie's *future* husband. They treated him like a son, perhaps better than his own parents ever had.

David said a prayer for the two lost souls there that night.

He climbed back into his car, tossing the flashlight onto the passenger seat, and hit the road once again.

Time wasn't on his side anymore. He raced to the hospital, breaking every traffic law to get to her in time.

The Reaper

THE END

9

The hospital was boarded up with police tape as the sun slowly rose up from the land. Ambulances and police cars, fire trucks – they had all lined up outside of the old hospital.

A crowd had gathered to see the commotion; news reporters had surfaced with their cameras, rolling footage on whatever had taken place earlier that night.

"This was a grisly scene," one reporter announced into a microphone.

Two men wearing heavy jackets that read CORONER across the back carried out a body in a black bag on a stretcher.

David looked stunned. He knew who was in that bag.

Maggie.

He pushed his way through to the front of the line. A tall black police officer doing crowd control was in front of him, asking people to go back to their daily routines. No one did, of course.

"Excuse me," he spoke to the officer. "Excuse me," he repeated louder.

He glanced at him.

"What happened here?" He didn't realize how trembling his voice was.

"A woman was murdered on the sixth floor," he said. "Margaret-something."

David backed up from the crowd and onto the street. He leaned against a squad car and planted his face in his hands. "God, no," he whispered into the wind.

He looked up at the building, staring at the sixth floor window, and there stood someone.

Something.

The figure looked over the crowd, as if he were judging them. His black robe was stained with dark splotches only visible from the circling lights of the emergency vehicles. It was as translucent as a ghost, and the silhouette disappeared and then reappeared. Shadows swirled in His presence. They were beneath Him and danced around the brick building in waves of joy.

That was her killer.

"I'm coming for you, you bastard!" David vowed to the phantom silently.

It disappeared like sand in the wind.

David ran after it, busting through the crowd and police tape, making a B-line for the door.

Amazingly, no one stopped him.

He was inside. He closed the door and threw the deadbolt.

A young cop pounded on the door and ordered him to vacate the premises, but he paid no mind and continued on his path to the sixth floor.

He took the stairs.

After climbing up five flights, it took a minute to catch his breath. Police officers and forensic experts gathered around one room. They snapped photographs and took swabs of evidence to bring back to their lab. But they weren't going to find anything. That was as obvious to David as the night was long.

He stayed out of their way, made sure no one saw him, and ducked behind the old reception desk each time a bobbing head pried away from the crime scene.

Over the radio, he could hear them calling. From outside, they warned that a man fitting David's description had entered the building and locked the doors.

One uniform cop went to check it out, exiting at the stairwell, as the others continued their work.

David waited and crouched beneath the desk. He listened. They were talking about clues and trace evidence and what kind of bastard could do this. But David knew that it was no man that had done this. It was something far worse.

The idea that Maggie was gone and never coming back hadn't sunk in yet. He wasn't sure when it would, but when it did, he'd break down and cry, quivering like a young boy afraid of a darkened closet in his bedroom.

Below him, on the ground, stained with a drop of blood, was a note from a small yellow pad. It was one of Maggie's. She carried that damn yellow pad with her wherever she went. She always told him, "You never know when you're going to need to leave a note behind." And she *had* left it behind, from the Beyond.

It was Maggie's handwriting – there was no mistaking it. He'd recognize her neat penmanship anywhere:

To stop it, the secret of the horsemen must be known. Find the secret and it will stop!

She knew that David would find it, and that he'd go to the ends of the world to find her.

He was still in awe, tears staining the note. He knew it was now his job to stop whatever Maggie had seen.

Though she hadn't wanted him involved in the mess she had stirred up, meddling in things too bizarre for her own grasp, Maggie had known he'd be there. She knew he'd hunt from one corner of the world to the other for her. Love made people do crazy things, he always thought. And this was no different. Or maybe it *was* different.

Holding the note tightly in his hand, David wiped the tears from his face and tried to put the pieces of this misshapen puzzle together.

The Reaper.

The Horsemen.

The Secret.

The more he stared at that stained piece of paper, the more reality was settling in.

The secret of the horseman *will* be known, Maggie, he silently vowed to her.

And David always kept his promises.

The Reaper

THE REAPER:
DARK FOUR

The Reaper

EMPTINESS
1

The sky was dark when the storm came in.

The air was frigid and dank, the night somber with thick snowflakes that passed through midnight until they became as fine as grains of sand.

David Bells sat in the living room, alone, no lights on in the house whatsoever. He gazed out the window at an empty street, and in his mind played and replayed images of Maggie Wilson. In his hand, he held the note. He always kept it on him, always in his pocket and always on his mind.

He hadn't quite figured out what had happened to Maggie that night at the old hospital, and perhaps he never would—but he made a promise to her when she died, and he wanted to honor his word one last time.

He slumped further in his recliner, sipping on a glass of Black Label to keep warm.

The unrelenting chill that traveled the length of his body was not from a draft, but from an inner frost that grew ice in his veins.

In the months following Maggie's death he'd thought about her a lot, even more than usual. It was a constant thing, like liquor is to an alcoholic. She was his addiction, but her addiction was something far worse. Her addiction got her killed in ways that David could not describe, and more often than not, refused to believe. He tried to drink away her memory, but the pain was always there; her smile, her face, her touch was always right in front him, and he hated it. He'd rather go on a drinking binge, cause a few brawls and get thrown in jail. Now, sadly, the bars were closed up for the night and wouldn't open until noon. He could wait until then. David had a cabinet full of liquor and a refrigerator that functioned better as a beer can dispenser than a place to keep food.

A photograph of Maggie and David sat on the end table. They looked so happy, peaceful, in high spirits that spring day at the beach in Northern New Hampshire. Her smile tortured him to the core of his soul. He probably should have packed it away in the darkest corner of his closet, buried forever.

Maggie's apartment had been rented out now, her stuff in a storage facility off Route 9. It had been there since the landlord had her belongings removed. David paid the movers and rental fees. He thought more than once about going by and clean it out. Get a smaller unit to lower the price, or just pack up some boxes and, with the photographs that decorated the walls in the hall and bedroom, cram it all in the back corner of the closet to be forgotten. He knew at least half her belongings could be trashed or given away, like clothes and shoes. He could just never bring himself to do it. It would mean she wasn't coming back. David couldn't live with the acute knowledge that Maggie was dead. Not yet.

The Horseman

What Maggie wrote stuck in his mind.

With his self-loathing pushed aside, he finished the last two fingers of scotch and fumbled the glass back down on the table, tipping it over and letting it fall to the hardwood floor. Like him, it shattered into miniscule pieces.

The phone rang.

He didn't bother to budge from his position. It was probably work or maybe just a telemarketer trying to sell something he didn't want to buy.

He read the note over again like he had at least a hundred times now. He hoped each time something new would pop out at him, leave him a clue.

It might never make sense to him; it might keep him wondering for a thousand years. But it was important to Maggie; it was something she had to have known David would figure out—or why leave a note at all?

The Reaper

He read it over and over again, another five times:

To stop it, the secret of the Horsemen must be known. Find the secret and it will stop!

There was something about the mystery of the words that kept David interested enough to hypothesis what they meant. And he thought Maggie must've kept notes about the meaning.

What better place to keep private notes than on a laptop.

David had packed it up in a box and taken it to the storage facility, wrapped in bubble wrap with the lid taped shut.

It was almost four in the morning, but he had to know.

He jumped out of his easy chair, a drunken shell of a man, and scurried to grab his coat and keys. He stumbled out into the cold, in the heap of snow, and got into his car parked in the driveway.

David looked back at the window and jumped at the voices he still heard from the night that he lost her.

The car was an icebox, the temperature close to single digits; the cold, much like the scotch, sunk into his bones, and like the hollow rush of the sea, the wind whipped against the frosty windshield.

Adrenaline pumped through his system, heart thumping like a jackhammer in the heat of a summer day. The

55

alcohol rushed through him and gave David the boost of courage he needed to carry out the deed. He stuffed the keys in the ignition and turned over the engine of his BMW. He yanked the handle and locked his hands on the steering wheel, trying to fight the drunken spell, but the damage had already been done.

I'm gonna regret this in the morning.

He forced himself to wait for the heater to defrost the windows. It only created a crevice in the center, enough to make eye contact with on the road, but not too many people would be riding around this late at night.

Maybe cops.

Shit, if I ever get pulled over…

He would have to concentrate even harder on the road, push aside the blurred vision, exhaustion and booze.

The car was a tad warmer than the outside elements, but the distinction between the two were very hard to tell. Clouds of breath still formed in front of his face as he backed out of the driveway onto the street, missing scraping his wheel on the curb by less than an inch.

Snowflakes spilled through the headlights, but while the rest of the world was lost in the utter darkness, shrouded by shadows, it was still just a blurred image to him. David was never the kind to drink and drive, but what had happened at the hospital—not to mention being questioned by the police for five straight hours until they finally released him with an apology—had changed a lot of things.

They had no leads; no leads and no suspects, and when that happened in such a grizzly case, the police liked to point a finger at someone. It was mostly political pressure. Someone always had to answer to someone else.

David was about ten minutes from the storage site. But to him, one street looked like another. He headed east down Oakwood, waiting for it to cut in, and turned right onto Mersk Road. From there he climbed on the highway, three miles and he cut off on exit seventeen. The storage facility was a mile up on the right.

David slowly eased the car into the right lane and turned. There were rows upon rows of storage lockers. He drove through an area marked WRONG WAY. It was narrow and barely fit the width of the car. He found Row 7 on the west part of the lot and parked in front of it.

He grabbed the keys from the ignition and stepped out on to a ground of virgin snow, leaving behind his footprints as he searched for locker 87. He fumbled for the key and held it tight in his hand. His walk was more like a stagger, and he leaned against the wall of lockers to steady himself.

He found it.

Locker 87.

He fit the key into the steel lock and it fell to the ground with a *clank*. He rolled up the door and searched impatiently for a cardboard box that had LAPTOP written on all sides of it.

He pushed clothes around, boxes with miscellaneous items in them, stuff that was probably fragile and needed to be handled with care, but he tossed them around as if they were pillows.

Underneath a small stack of boxes, probably now full of broken items, he found the box he was searching for. He barreled towards it, sending anything in his path to the cement floor. He carried the box under his arm and backed his way out of the eight-by-twelve-foot storage room, slamming the rolling door to the ground. He picked up the dropped lock and secured it. It was safe to go home again, throw back a few more shots and fall asleep in the recliner, which on most nights had become his bed.

Halfway home, he nearly drifted to sleep and swerved into the other lane, but regained control almost as fast. In the side mirror a pair of headlights came chasing in the dark. It was a good distance away, but he could tell it was a cop. The reflectors behind the hood, the slight view of overheads—*must be a damn cop.*

His street was the fourth one, and he sped past Sokeef Street and turned. The cop was too far behind to take notice.

Time to see what's on her computer.

David still had eighty-proof and his unshaven face and strewn hair made him look like a wino, but his appearance wasn't topping his list of concerns.

He wanted to make things clear, to understand what Maggie was talking about.

With all his heart, he believed that those answers rested within her computer.

IN SEARCH OF THE TRUTH COMES LIES
2

David unwrapped the computer on the kitchen table. He peeled the bubble wrap off and flung it to the ground. Grabbing the detachable cord, he connected it to the computer and then the wall socket.

He powered it on.

It was still cold and had not been used in months, but the welcome screen came on. No password required. He would've thought for sure that Maggie secured her files better than that.

David watched the green and blue lights on the front of the console flicker, stay steady, then flicker again.

He stumbled around, going from file to file and coming up with nothing but a few documents that seemed like research papers on the paranormal.

This must be it.

David read the first paper from beginning to end, over three hundred pages and nothing about Reapers or Horseman. The second document failed to open, instead prompting for a password. David stumbled through his thoughts and tried a dozen names and combinations of Maggie and her family, but he came up empty. He tried DAVID. The document opened like someone said the magic word.

David.

The file was much shorter than the last, and it was exactly what he was looking for. She left it for him to find the secrets. They looked like journal entries.

09/18/07

I finally figured it out, I think. I think? I don't know what to think any more. It's too hard to think. How can anyone think after what I just found out?

The only person, besides me that should read this file is David. I'm not sure if he'll get the chance to. I'm obviously dead or you wouldn't be looking at this. I'm not sure if anyone else will be around, either.

It's coming.

Something the world has feared for centuries is finally coming true. The only thing left to do is delay it as much as you can until the good comes.

I started by exploring the myths, mostly local because Massachusetts has a lot of history here. With history come ghosts.

And that's what I found everywhere.

Joseph McGee

They came to me in a dream.

I'm so scared. I've never been so scared before in my life, but at the same time I want to know more about Them. I want to know more about who they are, what they are, why they're here. I don't think there's really a lot I can say. It's something I know but can't quite put into words. There's not one, there's thousands. A whole race of them. And they all look the same: boney structure, a dark shrouded robe, and they all carry a scythe. I've seen the blades. They don't look like they've come from this world. They didn't. I know. But my God—it's still so surreal. It's like a nightmare I can't wake up from, and yet, all I want to do is go to sleep and pretend it's all just a horrible dream.

They're out there.

They crossed over the borders and now they're here. I don't know what they want, but I do know they're real. And they look like the perfect image of a Reaper.

10/18/07

The children are the worst.

I'm starting to see them now. They look so small and innocent, but with oily black eyes and pale skin, and I wonder if they were victims or hallucinations.

I still keep this diary going because I want someone to know I'm not crazy. These things do exist. And just because people choose not to believe does not mean I'm full of shit. I've seen them, walking around my house like they're fulfilling some ancient obligation, like they're still living their lives with purpose—ghosts.

They're everywhere. And when they sing in my head…the noise is just overwhelming. I can't hear myself think. They're in my head, in front of my eyes and in my thoughts.

They exist.

Everywhere.

The journal entries ended with three unmarked dates.

He read the text on her computer, allowed it to settle in, but he still couldn't believe it. He hadn't believed it even after seeing *it* for himself. Was what she was saying real, or did she finally fall off her rocker? There were so many questions left unanswered. The only person who could answer them was dead and gone, and the only thing David, a shell of the man he was, could do was go back there. Hunt down whatever it was and demand answers, demand the truth.

David shut down the computer, walked to the refrigerator and took out a bottle of water.

He braced himself against the countertop, looking at the dim kitchen and wondering how he let this happen to him, to Maggie, to Maggie's family. He never forgot that scene—their dead bodies sprawled on the floor after a horrific slaying he was too late to stop. He wanted to blame himself. He wanted to find some flaw in what he'd done that day to justify Maggie's death. He couldn't blame anyone, and that was the most frustrating part.

Months after being interviewed by the police, they still had no clues to any of the murders. David knew they wouldn't find any, either. The truth was far beyond any known law enforcement agency he could think of.

From the cabinet by the sink he grabbed a bottle of Tylenol, tossed three in his mouth and threw them back with a couple of slugs of water.

He would wait until morning. Right now, he had to nurse the onslaught of a massive hangover and pray he saw daylight once more.

Joseph McGee

Morning's Wake
3

The sun crept through the blinds, strong enough to wake David at just after nine in the morning.

So began the day that would change his life forever.

He rolled around in bed, fighting the pain throbbing in his head, the bitter taste in his mouth and the fact he wanted to stay in bed another week. But the sun wouldn't have it. Unlike an alarm clock, he couldn't smash the sun. The sun was one alarm that was relentless.

He forced himself to the edge of the bed and sat up. His bare feet touched the cold floor. Stumbling out of bed, cradling his forehead in the palm of his hand, he walked to the bathroom down the hall. He was tired and felt like he'd been run over by a Mack truck. His longer-than-normal hair was in disarray, sticking up like a warped porcupine. Heading into the kitchen, he took out the unfinished bottle of water from last night and realized the refrigerator was nearly empty save for rotten lunch meats and spoiled milk.

At nine forty-five he went to the living room and turned on the television for the news.

He sat in his recliner, still wearing nothing but his blue boxers.

His mind was not on the television, it was elsewhere, in an almost ethereal state. Even his headache seemed to dissipate long enough for a conscious thought.

Without thinking, he shut off the TV and went to his bedroom. Opening and closing drawers in his dresser, he pulled out jeans and a shirt and went to the bathroom for a shower.

The warm water washed over him, baptizing him in the new morning. He never really got up before noon anymore, staying up late and sleeping away the day. He hadn't written a single word for his publisher in months. He was still in good standing with the company, but if he put off his work too much longer, his status would definitely suffer. That was why he needed to finish this. He needed closure.

After the shower, he brushed his hair back out of his eyes and shaved his beard. In the mirror, he barely recognized himself. It was like staring at a complete stranger. And maybe that was good.

Someone walked by the door.

A child.

He went into the hall and looked both ways but saw no one. It was just a glimpse, a shadow, but he could've sworn he had seen someone pass by. He went back to the mirror and finished wiping the melting foam off his face.

It stared at him through the mirror. A child with black eyes, crying black tears.

The child in the mirror tilted its head.

"When the Reapers come to play, you better stay out of their way."

The glass exploded.

David covered his eyes with his hands. Shards of the mirror spiraled into his arms and chest, but not enough to cause serious damage, just to draw trickles of blood. He backed up until his naked back hugged the wall. Rattled, he dropped to the floor, cowering, still covering his face. Fear took over, but just for a moment before the anger flushed in.

He rose to his feet. It was a total transformation in real time. David's jaw was taut, teeth grinding; his eyes were wide and filled with fury. He walked out of the bathroom and grabbed his clothes hanging on the door. His shoes were strewn in the bedroom. After he laced them tight, he walked to the door to grab his coat, made sure he had his wallet and picked up the keys from the table.

The secret of the Horseman will be known.

He promised those words to her, and he kept his promises.

"I'm going to find out. I'm going to find what you are and how to…fucking…kill you." David slammed the door behind him as he left, stamping an exclamation on his words.

REVELATION
4

The library was quiet for a Monday morning. All the kids that patronized the place were in school; all the adults that came to catch up on their reading were at their jobs. It wasn't like the library was ever really crowded, but once in a while it was too busy for David's tastes.

He found himself in the Occult section. He ran down a list of titles, searching hard for something that resembled his problem. He ended up with six books; *Black Eyes, Hell's Crossing, Grim Reapers, How to Stop Evil Spirits, Do You Have Ghosts? Conquer Your Demons: The Real Kind.* It took him another minute to realize they were all by the same author, someone named *Michael Alexander.* He looked at the spine of the book, then the inside pages. They were self-published under the author's name. He was a local.

David carried the books under his arm and found a window-front table off to the corner. Outside the cars were moving steadily across the city through the slush and snow.

He turned the first book open.

Black Eyes.

Black-eyed children are common among myths. They are believed to be the children to the Grim Reaper himself, and while I'll get to Mr. Reaper later on, I must pay close attention to these children-like creatures, because they can enter your thoughts, they can manipulate you, confuse and destroy you all at the same time.

David read on for the next hundred and seventy-six pages of the hardcover spoof. It made for an interesting fable, but how real could it be? The back of the book was void of any information on the author save for: *Michael Alexander resides in Massachusetts where he continues to research and write.* Quickly he checked each book he had taken with him and it was the same line under the header ABOUT THE AUTHOR.

He wasn't looking to stalk the guy, but come on—what were the guy's credentials? What made him such an expert? Where did he get his information from?

It was just a smaller mystery in a universe of mysteries, David figured.

He turned to the pages of *Grim Reapers*.

It spoke not just about one entity but thousands. According to Alexander, a whole race of creatures commonly known as *Soultakers* existed.

David took the books off the table after another hour's worth of reading and checked them out at the front desk.

He had some heavy research to do, and a friend to get reacquainted with. Elizabeth Pierce.

Liz worked at the police department as a homicide detective. She was a good cop, but like most good cops, she fractured the rules a bit. She'd do this small favor for David—mum was the word.

By the time David returned home, a chill had snuck into the air that reminded him of his week-long getaway in the Alaskan Mountains. One of the three vacations he had taken with Maggie. The same ice was in the air, the same dankness and numbness. Feeling it triggered bullets of memory that ricocheted in his head. He embraced them, then dismissed them, refusing to allow painful memories to creep up.

Something about these ancient creatures seemed more real than myth. After all, ghosts and goblins, Dracula, the Jersey Devil and a throng of other mythical creatures had to originate from somewhere. Was it possible that a man could be so influential as to create lies big enough to leave the world in awe? *Maybe so,* he thought. *Maybe so.*

Later that night David lay stretched out on the sand-brown couch in his living room; he relaxed his head on the arm rest and drifted off to sleep with the glow of the television reflecting on the walls.

The room was dark, and so was his dream.

"They're here!" one man shouted over the scorching flames.

It was a church, the beginning of sunset as its red-orange rays lit through the doorways. The wooden pews were ablaze, men and woman were being burned alive, and all around them shadows circled with large scythes in hand. They wore dark robes that shielded their faces from the murdered souls. They spoke to each other in a foreign tongue that sounded a lot like a fat kid blowing a raspberry.

"Save your souls!" an older man, a priest judging from the robes, yelled.

The church turned to kindling. Twenty-six souls were lost, and each shadow-figure struck the gut of the dead with his blade and pulled them out, harvesting their souls.

The last one to die was the priest. They surrounded him behind the alter; above hung a five-foot crucifix of Jesus. One of them stepped forward. He railed his scythe once, and then plunged it into the priest. Blood seeped through the man's black coat and stained his white collar. His ribs broke. He cringed and fell to the ground.

David was there, but not corporeal. He was a ghost watching from a distance. He felt the heat from the flames like the summer sun. He watched on as the figures showed no remorse, stopped for no one, and allowed—no, helped—the church burn.

There were no sirens in the distance, no commotion he could hear from onlookers. David stood in the balcony, and walked to the window. It looked like rural Wisconsin. The houses were wood-and-frame buildings, the streets dirt. There wasn't a car in sight, but there was a man out front of his home a hundred yards away. His clothes were old-fashioned.

David felt a tightness in his chest, then dizziness, then he fell backwards gently.

David jumped from the couch, almost knocking the glass of Coke he had on his coffee table to the tan carpeting. He tried desperately to calm himself, but a panic attack had already set in. His lungs clenched, squeezed; long fingernails of fear scratched at his heart.

He reached to the phone on the end table and dialed Liz's cell.

"Pierce," she answered.

"Liz, it's David Bells. How you doing?" he huffed out.

"I'm doing good," she said, surprised to hear his voice. "You okay?"

"I don't know."

That gave it away. He wasn't *okay*, and like a good cop, Liz picked up on it.

"What's wrong, David?"

"So many things, Lizzy." He was fighting back tears, mustering up the strength to talk to her. His chin quivered and his stomach knotted. He was breathing between sobs. "That girl, from before."

"The one that was murdered?"

"Yeah. I think I know—I don't know. It doesn't make sense."

"David, what are you talking about?"

"Some shit's going down that can't—it doesn't make sense," he repeated.

"David, I'm going on my lunch break. Why don't I pick up some grinders and come over, okay?

"Sure."

"Tuna, tomatoes, lettuce?"

"Yeah. See you soon." He hung up and made his way to the bathroom to clean his face and force the panic out of his body.

He opened the door with a halfhearted smile.

"It's good to see you again."

"You too, David. It's been a while."

He ushered her to the kitchen, and she sat a large paper bag on the table. She was even more beautiful than he remembered. She stood nearly five-nine, with a mess of dirty blonde hair. She was the perfect image of a model. And a girl with a gun and handcuffs hit the spot for most guys, he supposed.

They talked over their sandwiches for the next half hour. For several minutes, while listening to David tell his story and checking the clock, she stared at him like she was back at the department in the interrogation room. She knew David, or used to back a while ago. But this seemed farfetched. Monsters? Demons? Hauntings? It was a good story, she thought, maybe one he was writing and was trying out on her.

But there was so much fear in his eyes.

"David," she half smiled, "what you're telling me can't possibly be true. Or is this something for a new book?"

"Liz, I know it sounds crazy." David got up from the chair, and walked to the sink with his hands behind his back. "I know you think I'm fucking losing it. Maybe I am. But I know what I saw. I know what happened. I saw it. And there's this guy and…"

"Calm down. I don't think you're nuts, but I do think that you've been through a lot lately."

"I need your help."

"With what?"

"I need to find someone."

"David, you know I can't do that."

"Liz, please. I don't know what else to do."

"You're scaring me"

"Lizzy, I'm fucking terrified."

"Who do you need to find?"

"This author. Michael Alexander. He lives around here."

Liz took a pad and pen from her back pocket and wrote down the name. "I'll see what I can do."

"Thank you," he said. "I know you don't believe, and that's okay, but please don't think I'm fucked up in the head. I need you to know I'm not losing my mind. Please."

"David, I don't think that." She paused for a moment, a deep breath escaping her. "Listen, I'll see what I can do, okay?"

David hugged her. "Thank you."

LIFE GOES; DEATH COMES
5

Every house holds both life and death.

Somehow it's trapped in time in a moment of confusion, like when someone's life is taken quickly, without warning. Their spirits linger on between this world and whatever comes next.

"Do you think it's true?"

"The stories? Maybe," Billy said.

"I don't like it here," Michael said.

"Don't be such a pussy."

"I'm not!"

"Then go in."

Michael looked on from the other side of the street at the abandoned hospital. The doors and broken windows were boarded up tight and the door, now a heap of splintered wood, had yellow tape across that warned POLICE LINE DO NOT CROSS. There were cracks in the wood, like tiny eyes watching the two teenagers. An eerie haze built around the grounds.

They'd heard the stories. *Everyone* had heard the stories. It was on the news and on the Internet.

The hospital looked as ferocious as a wild animal.

The chill in the air ran up through Michael's t-shirt and attaching itself to his chest. He wished he'd worn the hooded sweatshirt he'd left flopped over the kitchen chair.

Michael Bradley didn't want to show his fear, but it was pretty evident.

"What are you waiting for?"

"I'll go. Don't worry." He stepped off the curb and waited for a car to travel past him before heading for the other side of the road. "Prick," he muttered to Billy, but he had a feeling that his friend did not hear him, that his gaze was still stuck on the towering building. It seemed to loom over everything, including life itself; the shadows were scarce—and something moved on the rooftop.

Michael looked at the darkened sky and waited. Nothing came. Nothing moved again. He brushed it off, but he was scared.

He walked up the steps and knocked three times on what was left of the door. Good, hard poundings. Even in the dank air, he was sweating something awful; he'd start chewing on his fingernails if he hadn't already bitten them down as much as he could.

His world flipped when his knocks were answered.

The nailed boards rattled and screeched; from inside the compound, voices echoed, screaming to be heard. And all at once, in unison with a blood-curdling cry, the windows that were left exploded, raining glass onto the porch.

From in the darkness, a hand reached out and grabbed Michael's collar.

Billy ran down the street, eyes pooling with a black ink, reciting *The Reaper will come to play; The Reaper will come to play.*

The Reaper

In Twilight Lies the Waking Beast
6

"I'm sure there's some privacy law you broke to find me, Mr. Bells."

"I'm sure there is, sir. But like I said, I need your help."

"And why do you want to know about this?"

"My friend died because of it and I want to know why."

"Was it a reaper or did the horsemen just carry her to Hell?"

"*A* reaper?" He smiled. "I always thought only one reaper exists. The Grim Reaper."

Michael Alexander sat sprawled comfortably in his recliner in the living room; David sat opposite on the floral couch. Alexander spoke with a soft accent—British or Australian—it was too faint to tell. He was fifty-seven years old and seemed a bit too distinguished to be writing what others would call frivolous.

"I spoke the truth in each of my books, Mr. Bells."

"I believe you, but my friend's dead and I need answers. I need to know that I'm not going crazy."

Alexander sat with his legs crossed. He stared through beady eyes, looking David up and down, wondering if he *was* crazy. He'd gone through an absurd amount of trouble to track him down and was now speaking of reapers and his friend's death. It was a *Douglas Clegg* novel in the making, he thought.

"Mr. Bells, I don't think I'm the one to help you."

"You have to," David begged.

Michael Alexander breathed a deep sigh of regret. "Fine."

He stood from his chair. "Come with me."

David followed him through the kitchen and down to the basement.

The wooden steps creaked under their weight. Dust hung lazily in the air attacking, David's sinuses. The air was thick and dank, and the only light came from a single bulb dangling loose from the ceiling.

"Mr. Bells, the Grim Reaper is a myth passed down from generations at Halloween parties or in horror movies. He doesn't exist," he explained. "Instead of one reaper, there are thousands, possibly hundreds of thousands."

David listened as he followed the man to the far back corner of the basement and into a room that wasn't much larger than a closet. It was a tight fit for one man, let alone both of them. Three four-drawer filing cabinets lined one wall, and a chipped and mangled desk sat in the corner with papers neatly pressed into stackable slots beside a computer monitor.

He sat in a small wooden chair that would've better fit the needs of a child than a man pushing sixty.

"So what you're telling me is that reapers are a race?"

"Oh, yes. Very much so."

"How do I kill them?"

"The question you need to ask is can anyone really kill anyone?"

"I don't need fucking riddles," David lashed out. "I want answers. I want to find out what the hell happened."

"You want that, but do you need it?"

David's face turned a soft red from aggravation. He wanted to rip off this hack's balls and shove them down his throat along with his pompous attitude. He leaned his weight against the unfinished doorjamb; wood splinters rubbed off on his black shirt, as did dust from layers of sheetrock that had been amateurishly put together.

The ground consisted of dirt and a thick layer of rocks; spiders lurked in every dark corner, earthworms slithered on through the dampness and a family of rats had found refuge from the cold and stormy nights.

Alexander pulled a keyboard from behind the paper trays and brought up a file. Almost immediately documents began to pile up in a digital folder.

"You asked how to kill them, right?"

"Yes."

"There's only one way."

"What is it?"

"Be patient," Alexander said. "You won't win. No one ever does."

"Well, I have to try."

"So did the ones before you."

Alexander printed the files.

"I don't know how true it is. It's really just a rumor, Mr. Bells."

"What is?"

"The legend of reapers goes far back. The Devil needed collectors of souls, and with each population of this world and its infinite number of parallel worlds, he created a race of soultakers, known as reapers. To collect someone's soul, a reaper must use his scythe to cut from their body. They're made of solid silver, except for one." He paused for a moment, watching the printer stop. "I found this—and I must repeat: by rumor—from a book that was allegedly written by a high-ranking demon centuries ago; a book known to cults and Satanists and people with peculiar hobbies as Necromancer. It says that the eldest reaper, the first one created has a scythe that is made of solid iridium."

"Iridium?"

"It's an extremely rare metal from the platinum family, but it's much more expensive and hard to come by. I understand it can withstand the fires of Hell up close. They say stealing that particular scythe and using it on the eldest of reapers would destroy them all."

David looked into Michael Alexander's eyes, but couldn't tell if he was speaking the truth or just a crazed man with—as he put it—a peculiar hobby.

"And what does iridium look like?"

"It's heavy and thin. Silvery-white like a pearl."

Alexander stood up from his chair, walked to the printer and waited for the final pages to sprout out from the machine. He handed a stack of at least a hundred pages to David. "This is all you should need to fulfill your quest for answers and find closure."

Closure?

He was damn sure not looking for closure.

He wanted revenge.

From that moment on, David knew his life was nearly over, that it would never be the same again. But if someone like Michael Alexander had gone to him with a portfolio and explanation of his demise, it wouldn't have stopped him.

Alexander led the way back upstairs to a now darkened home. A veil of gloom had settled in.

David, though annoyed with Alexander's attitude, thanked him for his time as he left. Outside the storm began.

In the Heart of Madness
7

The two boys were standing in the back of Saint Augustine's Cathedral on Drake Street. Across the road was a twenty-four hour mini-mart, a place known for drug use and violence. Vincent Kennedy and Ryan Harper crouched behind the trunk of an '87 Toyota in rusted blue.

Ryan had dragged Vincent along to score some PCP from Sledge.

Neither of them knew the dealer's real name, but they didn't spend much time worrying about it. He was called that because of the way he dealt with problems—a sledgehammer to the skull. Once, he had used it to crush a man's genitals for screwing him over twenty bucks. The man was too afraid to press charges even when the cops grilled him for several hours. Sledge's reputation preceded him. It was the nature of the street.

Ryan had dropped a fifty for his fix, and they were headed back to his house when something in the back of the church caught their attention. It was too dark to see, and had it not been for the neon signs at the Laundromat and a dim streetlight, they probably wouldn't have seen anything. As it was, they both prayed they hadn't.

88

People were there, seven or eight, cloaked in dark robes. More disturbing was the fact they seemed to be floating, not walking, the robes only shifting in the wind and not with their weight. They held large wooden objects with a curve of metal at one end. In the middle, on bended knees was a black woman, topless, crying and pleading to not be harmed. Her breasts were bare and bloody from lacerations across her cheeks and jaw; little dribbles of blood ran from the crevice in her lips and gums. Her life was over. Ryan and Vince both knew it as they watched on in horror, much like children watching a scary movie, unable to peel their eyes away for a second.

One of the shrouded figures broke from the circle and looked down at his prey. He raised his scythe in the air, slammed it in her and ran it across her stomach.

The loose skin of her belly flapped open and blood and fluids spilled to the ground.

It began to rain.

Ryan and Vincent fell flat to the ground to avoid being seen by the cloaked men or the mini-mart employee through the barred windows. Vincent was cold and not wearing much but a t-shirt with a flaming skull in the middle. Ryan wore a jacket-vest and stained jeans. Underneath the car, they peered and watched the group stand in a straight line.

In the darkness they heard a trotting sound, like horses carrying along in a parade; their whistles and grunts carted in the wind. As if from nowhere, four cloaked figures on horseback rode into the back of the church.

One of them got down and used a thick rope to bind the dead woman's arms and tied it to the satchel attached to the back of the horse. For a split second, Vincent could've sworn the figure he saw was no man at all, that when his hood had scrunched down, he saw a bare white skull.

"Let's get the fuck out of here," he whispered to Ryan.

"No. They'll see us." He pulled Vincent closer to refute any idea he had of running down the street screaming. In that neighborhood, people would bolt the doors, lock the windows and pray that ricocheting gun fire wouldn't break the windows.

"You kids shouldn't be here," a voice whispered from behind them.

Frightened, they turned their heads slowly and saw a man dressed in black combat attire, shotgun in hand. He shouldered the gun and walked out beside them. "Go back into the store. Don't come out."

They stood slowly, trying to keep concealed behind the parked car before they disappeared into the store. Confusion and fright were plastered on their faces.

David Bells cocked the shotgun and hurried through the shadows to the church.

He crept alongside the building, slowly edging his way to the back lot of the church, where four hundred years ago a high priest had sanctioned the place to be a breeding ground for the devil and his minions.

David lowered the gun and saw the dead woman sprawled on the pavement with her ankles tied to the saddle of one of the riders. Two of them had rode off not five feet and vanished into a field of overgrown weeds, the third and fourth riders about to do the same.

He fired a round into the line of reapers, not caring which one took the brunt of the blast. He fired a second round, then a third and fourth. Each one had no effect, but they turned, their glowing yellow eyes speaking fury to David's soul. He fired one more time into the ground.

He ran, using the shotgun as leverage to power through the reapers, and like a defensive tackle, pushed his way through as a scythe slid down his back. He growled from the hot streak of pain, but adrenaline kicked in like a shot of whiskey. His heart was racing louder and faster than he thought was humanly possible. He dove on top of the woman's body as the rider dragged her behind, disappearing in the night, David Bells going along for the ride.

Ryan and Vincent finally got the female store clerk to call 911. Their frantic ramblings convinced the clerk perhaps that time she wasn't dealing with just another junky kid.

If they were high, why the hell would they want the police to come?

A few minutes later, four cruisers pulled up, flanking the church, followed by an unmarked car with flashing blue lights on the dash.

A woman entered the mini-mart where the two witnesses waited; her gun holstered, her gold shield hanging loose around her neck from a ball link chain.

"Detective Pierce, these are the two witnesses."

"Thank you." She turned to the two teenagers. "There's a lot of blood across the street but no body—want to tell me what happened?"

Ryan looked at her, thoughtfully. "Lady, you're not going to believe this."

"Try me," she said.

Horrortown

It all started about two months ago, when this new family came to town, into our quaint little neck of the woods—Braston, Mississippi. No one believed me, but I bet they believe me now and are kicking themselves in the ass for not listening to me when they had the chance to change things.

My name's Mike Stole. I'm an architect. I've been very successful at what I do, so successful I decided to take a year off and spend it with my family. It really beat staying in the den every day looking at blueprints until my eyes went numb some time around two o'clock in the morning. And my family is very important to me.

That brings me to another family.

Theodore Scott, his wife Madeline, and their twin daughters, Amy and Ashley, were strange to say the least. The twins always wore the same clothes, and it might've been cute at age five, but not at thirteen. They had bleach blonde hair, a few shades darker than chalk, and smiles...oh, smiles that could make your skin crawl. After they moved into the old mansion on Bucker Street, nothing was ever quite the same.

Scott looked like a business man, and had the suit to match. One of those five-hundred-dollar jobs, from a place with an Italian limerick for a name. He carried a briefcase, and drove off in his Audi every morning at eight-thirty sharp, like clockwork. I doubt there was ever a day when he was late for his job, whatever it was. You see, I never found out too much about them before everything got all screwed up. I never knew about his job. I wasn't stalking him or rummaging through the garbage when the wife would take the girls into town for school.

Madeline was a housewife, staying at home and watching the kids after they got out of school, at three-fifteen each afternoon.

Amy and Ashley never played with the other kids, or so my boy tells me. My son, Eric, is in the same class as the twins, and he's terrified of them. It was something in their eyes, he'd tell me. There was some part of them that was so malevolent and manipulative, like they were born without souls, dominions of Evil.

But hopefully he was afraid of something other than the ramblings he may have overheard.

That's the funny part.

I just started having these dreams about the time *they* moved in, I began to have nightmares, and talk in my sleep. Nightmares of a town of horror.

And when I told my wife, I called it Horrortown.

There was really nothing else to name it. It was just a place in my mind where the worst of the worst could become reality, and it looked an awful lot like my neighborhood, only at the end of the world.

Let me take you back to the beginning, where this will all make much more sense.

Now, I don't want you to think I'm fifty kinds of fool, but this is true, as true as anything here on Earth can be. It's a way of belief I suppose. The way some believe in God and some don't; the way some believe in paranormal phenomenon and some think it's poppycock.

Anyway, let's go back. Let me get you up to speed.

It was the third day of June, and one hell of a hot spell was brewing. No rain for weeks—drought is the only word that comes to mind, famine too. It must've been pushing ninety-five degrees that afternoon.

I noticed the moving van at the top of the hill, a few blocks from my home. It was idling by the sidewalk, with three men outside carrying furniture and a fourth in the back unloading boxes. I drove by on my way to the mini-mart.

When I left for the store something terrible was brewing in the sky, an uncalled for thunderstorm. The meteorologist hadn't mentioned anything about it last night on the eleven o'clock news.

"What a goddamn liar," I cursed to myself as I climbed into my car and fired up the ignition. There was a good chance rain was on its way, and it would be good for the farmland out in Desishaw County. They could really use it.

Before putting the car in drive, I twisted the cap off the bottle of cola I'd just bought, and placed the ten scratch-tickets in the passenger seat. Sometimes I have the urge to test my luck with a handful of scratch offs every now and then. It's a foolish habit, like smoking cigarettes, only there's no chance of dying from losing a few bucks in the lottery.

A hard hammer of rain pelted my windows. Rain so hard it echoed off of my roof with a series of *thuds*. I looked out my windshield into the blackened sky, searching for a piece of haven—a lonely beam of sunlight trying to break its way through, but it was as dark as my black Escort.

I drove home with the wiper blades swatting the water away from the glass at full speed, and just like in some redundant horror movie from the seventies, peering at me from the top window were those little girls, as if they knew I was coming this way and wanted to make a special appearance on my behalf.

When I pulled in my driveway I could have sworn I saw them again in my yard, soaked with rain in their pretty white dresses, patterned with flowers, and their golden hair streaming with water and dripping mercilessly. But I opened the car door, trying to avoid the rain, and their ghostly images disappeared into the wind.

It wasn't until later that evening that things blew up, though.

Eric was staying at a friend's house. Dillon was just a week younger than my son, and they'd been best friends since first grade; his parents lived only three houses away from the mansion, which worried me, but I trusted my son with them as they trusted Dillon with me and my wife.

I got the call a few minutes shy of midnight. Eric sounded panicked, as if he were panting like an expectant father in a waiting room, nervous and scared. He was out of breath, and I could tell that he was frightened by something or someone. After he pleaded with me to come get him, I left without even leaving a note for my wife. She was at her book club, like every Friday night, and on rare occasions, she'd stay until midnight or later doing whatever it was she did down there.

I rushed over to the Tanner's. The front door was open.

I found Mr. And Mrs. Tanner dead, strewn about in a bloody heap, as if some kind of explosive device had been detonated, but left no scorch marks on the crust of their dismembered parts.

Slashes marked their bodies like a thousand paper cuts; Matt Tanner appeared to have been reaching for the shotgun he kept in his office, but whoever killed him did it before he could turn the key in the hole.

"Eric!" I screamed out once, twice, three times. I didn't hear any response. I turned on the lights in the living room, checked around the furniture, in the bathroom and kitchen but couldn't find a soul. I ran upstairs as fast as my legs could carry me, fearful my son had suffered the same fate, and was now lying in a pool of his own blood.

In Dillon's room, I saw them. Those two little witches—and witches they most certainly had to be, whether literal or not—they were wicked, nonetheless.

He was afraid they possessed some supernatural power, willing the most heinous acts on someone, or even killing them, probably with a single thought.

I could hear the thunder outside. Clear as ever. It was like an echoing god, calling out names in judgment.

But why would they attack my son? This family? There was nothing to gain by killing these people.

Something grander was happening there, and I knew it. I could see it in them, hear it in the heavens. I saw the purest and brightest lightning strike the ground in anger.

They weren't after money and it wasn't the joy and pleasure of one's suffering. They wanted the town to themselves. With unimaginable powers they could rule anywhere—everywhere. It reminded me of an episode of *The Twilight Zone* where a single child possessed the ability to make any object disappear with his thoughts. It was something not of this world.

The look of them made my face cringe in pure horror, like watching *The Shining* for the very first time.

The twins stood over my son's body. His chest was rising and falling. He was still alive. His friend—or what was left of him—was scattered behind him, brain matter trickling down the blue wall. His head had exploded from the inside. A single eyeball rolled by the bookcase where Dillon kept his *Goosebumps* collection near the window.

Lightning fell from the heavens and scorched the grass outside, then an earth-shattering rumble of thunder, like a detonated bomb.

Blood soaked the carpet.

Dillon's intestines spilled to the ground in a gooey mess.

The smell of death filled the room so quickly it was difficult to breath, like something was clenching my lungs. Tears welled in my eyes. I was scared for him. I wanted to trade places with him.

In unison they said, "We know that you know. And knowing is very deadly."

The sweet and innocent voices made them even more terrifying somehow.

Amy and Ashley were normal girls, or so it seemed, dressed nicely as if they were attending a formal party. Hair tied back in pony tails, their wicked smiles enjoying the torture they were casting upon my son and me, the joyous giddiness they seemed to take in killing people.

"What do you want?" I said in a hostile voice.

And why shouldn't I be hostile? They had my son at their feet, unconscious.

"What did you call it?" the left twin asked.

"Horrortown," the other answered.

"Isn't that what you said to your wife? Isn't that what's in your dreams?"

How the hell would they know what's in my dreams or what I said to my wife?

"Don't hurt my son, you cunts!"

"That language is unbecoming," they said simultaneously. "Your son will not be harmed. These people have not been harm…"

"No, they're just dead," I interrupted.

"To you, yes, they are dead," the left one said.

"To us, they're very much alive," said the right one.

Their eyes glowed black for a brief moment, and like fins they shut, closed like they had two different sets of eyelids; one vertical and one horizontal.

"What is it that you want?" I asked

"We want a place where we belong," they said together. "Your *Horrortown* will become our home."

And I remembered the dream, vivid, as if it were real and right in front of me, as real as the night sky displaying an ocean of stars: mass chaos, the destruction and the macabre that came with their need to feel welcomed.

"Mommy and daddy were the first," the right one said, and then the left one picked up, "and you'll be the next."

"The next what?"

They pointed to the window. I still kept a close eye on my son, wanting so desperately to go near him, to take him home with me.

I realized it then.

I pushed aside the blinds on the window and saw for myself, saw with my own two eyes, with no deniability.

This was *Horrortown*.

ONLY DEATH WAITS ON THE OTHER SIDE

The moon gleamed in his eyes. He stared and waited, stared across the frozen lake to the other side. He smiled halfheartedly. The moonlight in the country revealed the sleeping trees and a critter that raced through the underbrush staying undetected by its superior on the food chain, until… some creature of the woods wrestled it to the ground and the dying cries of the animal blessed the night.

Just as he was about to do.

The voice lifted out of the darkness, "Don't hurt yourself."

"I won't."

Eddie Baxter fooled around with the electrical box and flipped the switch. The lights came on all at once. "Told you I could fix it."

"We need the heat, it's freezing outside."

"Turn it on now, it should work." He closed up the box in the hall.

The power had gone out some thirty minutes ago in the wake of a blistering snowstorm just outside of Kittery, Maine, where things can get quite chilly if the power ever happens to go out on you. He stocked up on fuses and supplies just in case of something like this. He was like that. He'd made the spare closet in the hall something of a supply cabinet, making sure they could live comfortably for a month or so in case a bad storm ever made its way in and the county roads had to close down; canned food, bottled water, spare blankets. It's not like the State Police ever made it out this way to warn people with their little hole-in-the-wall cabins that a big, nasty blizzard was on the move; any cop who'd drive out here to do that would be fucking crazy.

The dead have highways, and for Eddie he was dealing with his own death. After their son died four years ago from a terminal illness, he'd never been quite the same. He had stuck it out with Terry only because he knew he would never find another woman to love him in his state of mind. She was dealing with Steven's death too, but in her own way. She still had a life. She went to dinner with her best friend, Tanya, saw her sister and niece almost weekly and made it to see her parents every Sunday for dinner.

This little slice of nowhere was the perfect place to relax, Eddie thought. Their little nook in the woods. No one to bother them but Mother Nature, and even she was being a bitch right about now, with gusts of wind blowing fierce, frosting up the windows, the echoes of whimpered cries slashing through the eaves.

Terry had never seen a snowstorm quite like this before. She was born and raised in a sleepy town outside of San Antonio before she met Eddie twelve years ago. He'd been on a business trip, trying to sell an advertising campaign to a new line of pet products. He'd nailed the deal, which gave him a large bonus and a corner office at Mercy & Bailey Advertising in Boston. He was very successful in his time there, but after Steven had died, he lost touch with his creative side and it suddenly became about death. Every add campaign had a slogan full of suffering. Subtly, there was always demise in some form or fashion, and that quickly brought him to the end of the line, ultimately costing him his job. Last spring he had started his own small marketing agency that fared well with the mom and pop shops in the town but never really mustered up enough money for two people to live on. Terry took a job working as a manager in a department store just across the border in New Hampshire. It kept her mind off of Steven. She didn't dwell around the house all day with leftovers and daytime television that seemed more real to her than her actual life anymore.

Eddie threw a few more logs on the fire.

He'd opened the door, stepped out onto the porch and rustled up some twigs and sticks that had wandered their way over and threw them into the crackling fire, drying the wood from melted snow and scorching it until they became ash.

They sat on the sofa in front of the fireplace looking out the window at the night sky and watching the snowflakes grow larger with each floating plunge. It was a beautiful sight, looking out at the Great Beyond, a storyteller's imagination perhaps, or just a wonderful movie.

He knew about Steven. He was the reason for his death.

He had no quarrels with Eddie or Terry Baxter. It was a simple infection he had inflicted. It was supposed to work, dammit! The infant, at birth, was to carry a dormant disease. He called it *The Inhuman Condition*, naming it after a Clive Barker novel that seemed to make more sense to him than this real world. It was the illusion that he was in love with.

Four years after the death of Steven, Michael Rindonour was still worried it might get back to him, that all his years of research and endless nights digging up the souls long forgotten by time would come to an end once the world figured out who he is and what he'd been up to these past few decades. He had no doctorate of any kind; he dropped out of Yale in his third year to pursue his bizarre endeavors. Only one classmate knew of his plans and threatened to alert someone of his scheme. That was Julie McGraw, the girl he loved. He murdered her one night with an overdose of household chemicals and a set of slit wrists. The Medical Examiner's office ruled it a suicide. If he was willing to kill someone he entrusted and gave his heart to, a couple of strangers wouldn't stand a chance.

There was nothing particular about him that made him stand out. He was five-ten, one-sixty and had no abnormalities or scaring. He wore a brown leather coat, a fleece sweater and a pair of dungarees.

Michael never believed in guns. They were too loud and, frankly, they scared him. Michael wasn't an evil man; he just carried out evil deeds. He had workman's gloves on, the kind you buy at a hardware store for heavy lifting; the knife he used was purchased—more or less illegally—at a flea market about an hour away in Grafton, Massachusetts. He bought it from an Asian man selling it underneath the table (in the glass cases were pocket knives with blades no bigger than your palm, various colors and designs made them all unique). This was a modern day machete. He had used it once before. Julie.

It was time to be used again.

He lifted the blade to his nostrils, inhaling the smell of steel and the copper smell of crusted blood—Julie's blood. He sniffed long and hard like a drug addict snorting a line. He had to get the scent from the overpoweringly dank air.

Once he went past the frozen lake to the cabin, there was no turning back.

Only death waited on the other side.

It only mattered to the sun.

Eddie and his wife hadn't had any type of intimacy in more than a year. Maybe they felt guilty, or maybe they didn't want to accidentally have another child in fear the same fate that bestowed their son would continue with their next child. It was a rare disease that their doctors had never seen before, and if Eddie didn't have the kind of funding he had saved from being the advertising genius that he was, they wouldn't have been able to pay for Doctor Abdu Gekahil all the way from Africa. He and a select group of doctors were the few to ever be present when the disease took control of a child's body. He was only seven years old at the time. It was a disease that ate away at his organs all at once, slowly, as if his body didn't belong in this world, that it could not adapt to our way of life; the air, the scents, the allergens, the people seemed to make his condition worse. It was like transporting a child to another dimension far more complex than his natural habitat. And in short, his days of activity got shorter and shorter until seeing the doctor was a weekly routine—praying an hourly one.

In each other's arms, the time seemed to go by slowly as their eyes grew tired listening to the wavering winds of snowfall and the warmth of the fire before them; they were comfortable enough to sleep right there.

The bedroom was upstairs and already fixed for the company of two. The fireplace in the bedroom had been burning, but by now it would probably be dying out. Their main source of heat came from electric heaters, one in the upstairs hall and the other in the kitchen. A fireplace only did so much, but if the electricity were to burn out again, they could simply scavenge enough wood and lock themselves in the bedroom, occupied by a good book and blankets.

From outside, he watched through a pair of binoculars. He zoomed in on the left portion of the house, through the window and into the seating area where he saw victims number three and four, waiting for their eyes to draw heavy before he could sneak around the lake and end it once and for all. There was no telling exactly what they knew or even if they knew anything at all. Michael did not want to take the chance.

He was never in control of the situation; after all, he was not the one that infected the baby. It was Something That Shall Not Be Named. It was a powerful being that Michael called upon, and in his wake, he needed living, breathing babies to be born upon. He needed to take human form and develop, over eighteen years, his already unparalleled powers.

He found a book in a secondhand store with torn pages and a creased cover. What fascinated him was the title of the book—*The Book of the Untold*. It was on a clearance rack because of its poorly kept condition, but as Michael skimmed through a dozen pages, he knew it was exactly what he needed.

It was a winter demon. A demon that could make snow cover the earth in whole, be swallowed by ice; Michael couldn't care less about this world he lived in, and besides, he'd read enough to know that if you summoned things from another world it would *almost* never do you harm, so long as you kept your end of the deal. Michael planned to keep his contract with the beast.

The first time he had laid eyes on him was out near Lynn, Massachusetts. A small community with not a lot of activity, and definitely not a metropolitan area. And the perfect place to summon a monster from the pits of Hell. In doing so, he released a force so much greater than this world had ever seen. The snowstorms were merciless; the authorities were finding bodies frozen stiff as if they were in an incubation chamber to be iced over like popsicles. It was a horrible thing to unleash on the world, and Michael did not know of its true power until the day it demanded the life of a child, so that it may live in that body for an eternity.

Michael would not release the creature on his own son or anyone he cared about. Choosing the Baxter child was merely chance, like tossing a coin up and calling heads or tails.

Steven Baxter was sleeping peacefully in the nursery of the hospital when Michael pricked him with a needle and pushed the clear liquid into his system. It implanted thoughts and memories into the child, rearranged his genetic makeup as if he were created in a lab instead of born from the love of two people.

He thought to himself while shoving his hands deep in his denim pockets, *this is it. Now or never. They might know what I've done to their son. They might—*

A hoarse rasp from behind caught him off guard. He drew his blade upward, ready to come down across the face of whatever unsuspecting bastard was at the wrong place at the wrong time—or maybe it was…Him.

It was an animal. A raccoon, he thought, but it was too dark to make out the fury details. It scattered off in the night, startled by Michael's sudden movement.

He held the knife at his side and peered once more through the binoculars that hung from his neck.

It was time.

Michael Rindonour traveled around the lake to a small rope bridge that seemed out of place. The ropes were ripped and worn. The wooden walkway was rotted and cracked. He took his time crossing. He knew death was waiting on the other side.

"I'm tired," Terry said. "I think I'm going to go upstairs and call it night."

"Okay," Eddie said tiredly. "Guess I'll go, too."

"I miss him."

"I know," he said. "Me too."

Once in a while she would blurt out a comment about their son, how she missed him, that she still loved him and would die to bring him back and hold him for one final moment. She knew that day would never come, but with all mothers, a special bond was formed at birth, a bond no one else could share with their child, as if their psyche was connected on some higher level. She always believed that he was still out there, somewhere. Even after the funeral, when they laid poor Steven into the ground, she believed that one day he would come back to her. Maybe she was just naïve, maybe just heartbroken, or maybe she knew something no one else could possibly know: Steven was still out there somewhere, calling out for his mother, alone and scared.

The bedroom was dark save for the flickering of the fireplace dancing on the walls, swaying in motion. The bedroom was neatly kept. The windows on the farthest side of the room showed the wicked weather howling and cursing its hatred, slapping clouds of fresh snow harshly against the glass. The cold wind rattled and then fell silent. Eddie tossed a couple more logs on the fireplace from the stack off to the side of the homemade two-tier unit he'd built the year before.

Eddie had taken up carpentry as a way to release his frustration and anger. He could hammer the hell out of a nail and pretend it was anyone he wanted.

The idea that Spring was only a couple of months away seemed like a dream, as if winter was all that existed and snow was all that was known. It swept down in whistling tidal waves, exhausting itself against the cabin; knocking on the doors, rattling the windows, tapping on the roof, like footsteps of Santa Claus, as mythical as the coming of spring seemed to be.

They had placed themselves in ordinary fashions, taking turns using the bathroom, brushing their teeth and getting ready to call it a night.

They'd been sleeping in the same bed, less than an arm's length from one another, but they didn't touch—it would've been too much for either of them to handle.

Lying beneath the wool blankets on the mattress, Eddie Baxter had thoughts racing through his mind of who his son would be today had he not died the horrible, agonizing death he did. He would've been four years old, just learning how to ride a bike, starting to see that girls really didn't have cooties, learning how to swim for the first time. There were so many first moments they were robbed of, so many memories never made, wearing the pain like a heavy coat. Steven was a story left untold, a novel with the ending ripped out.

The door creaked open slowly. He walked in, gently closing the door behind him. He had what it took to kill again; that gleam in his eyes, passion and desperation mixed together in a sadistic cocktail. There was no way out. No other alternative.

No reason was ever brought to Michael's attention that either of the boy's parents were snooping around or asking that their baby be dug up from his grave, and by now the body should've been well enough decomposed to cover the puncture wound from the needle in the back of the neck. He didn't want to take the chance. He *couldn't* take the chance.

For a brief moment the snowflakes chasing each other down the living room windows caught his attention. The whiteness that glittered outside shifted inward, illuminating a soft haze around the downstairs.

"It's now or never," he whispered to himself, trying to build up the courage to do it again.

The downstairs had beautiful architectural structure. Paintings hung on the walls, the cheapest of which was probably a grand or so. It was the way they lived, he thought. They, like everyone else on the planet, wanted to feel relaxed and comfortable, but not everyone can afford a two-story cabin with a couple of fireplaces and a couple of bathrooms and thousand-dollar paintings hung for the sake of color.

Michael shuddered.

Beside the lamp on the end table, he saw a picture of Eddie and Terry when she was pregnant with Steven. He saw her glow, their smiles—they were a family for a distinct moment, but now they'd drifted to nothing more than tolerable roommates.

Still, it must be done!

The stair case sat in between the small kitchen and living room. It led to the hallway. Only a bathroom and the linen closet stood to the right.

He heard footsteps, then a muffled gasp that sounded like a cry for help.

Michael Rindonour, pale face, shaky knees and all, pulled the blade and held it at his side, muscles tightening and hand taut around the handle.

He walked in cautiously. The room was doused in blood, from the white wool sheets to the varnished walls. The blood smeared on the floor and splattered on the walls like squeezing a ketchup bottle.

Terry was dead.

Her throat was slit, cutting through an artery that exploded on the wall in gruesome flavor; the flaps of skin looked like fish gills, still swaying in the motion of a soft, gentle breeze perhaps induced by the fire, or by a draft from the window.

He scanned the room. Saw nothing but the dead body.

"I knew you'd come back," a voice said from the shadows. When it emerged, it carried the lifeless body of Eddie Baxter—only part of him. His legs still remained on the floor, but the rest of him was intact, except for his jaw, which was hanging by shreds of skin. He managed to knock it loose from his head with one clean strike. Blood poured from his open wounds.

This was no man. This was Him. The Beast. The Thief of Life. A hundred other names given to Him. It was a winged monstrosity; skin shit-brown, eyes as black as the abyss of space. It had a mouth like a dragon, a snout like a dog, and wings like a bat.

And it killed for fun.

"How did…"

"Forget how," the raspy voice demanded. "You summoned me, you petty bastard."

The Beast took a deep breath and blew a cold, liquid breeze that cemented his hand.

Michael's face lost its color, and he fell to the floor, shattering his right arm into pieces that sparked in the fire and shot out in an explosion of flames with The Beast's laughter.

Michael cried out, though the sight was far worse than the pain. He fell into shock. The Beast grabbed him by his leather belt strap with one arm and tossed him into the fireplace. The flames engulfed him, sucked him in and melted his flesh, and the last things to burn were his heart and brain. The stench of death was overwhelming. It carried outside as the fire sparked to the bed, the floor, and the furniture. It was spreading fast and furious, like Michael's dying screams.

The Beast, still carrying Eddie's half-body, flung it through the window as it flew out; reaching above the treetops and watching the smoke wither lazily into the night's sky.

119

They were all dead.

The Beast was free.

With one quick swipe of his hand, the frozen lake below parted like solid waves of water. He retreated slowly into the great beyond of whatever lay below.

And death waited on the other side.

The Reaper

THE NIGHTMARE TRAIN

Nightmares have highways.

They run like ghost trains through your mind and across the wastelands of your thoughts, dragging departed souls from one world to the next in an endless traffic. Nightmares always find a way to make themselves come true; you can hear them shout out your name through the cracks in the world, listening to you as you cry out for some sort of salvation that you know will never come. And just as it nears the end, just when you can take no more punishment, you want to take a pistol to your head and pull the trigger—goodbye.

I don't have that luxury.

I'm on that Nightmare Train, probably going through your mind right now and tearing something up like raw meat through a grinder and mashing it back together. Some would call it a gift from the deepened snowfields of the otherworld. I mean you no harm, but harm is all I know; I'm the conductor of this maddening circus ride. And my next stop is your worst fear.

Don't blame me for what I'm about to do. It's the Hell that has brought me back to life from the place where the deceased's voices are the most shrill and battered. I bring them to you, not for simple revenge for an unkind act you once committed, or for something you may do later on in life. I'm not here for you to help out orphans or donate money to the homeless. I'm simply here to collect fears, to collect your nightmares and make you live through them until you finally snap and reach the breaking point, the point where things get a bit funky, the wires in your head get a little crossed and routed. Then you're a feeble man who can't even wipe himself.

Don't blame me.

I'm just a soldier in these Night Wars. I'm one of many. If it wasn't me, it would be someone else.

I come from a place that's known to you as Hell. We call it home. And before you think of it as a city surrounded by fire and death, let me correct you. It's cold sometimes. Very cold. Our snowstorms can go for months on end. We don't measure in inches, but in feet. Last week was a fourteen-foot blizzard coming down from the mountaintop of Thunder Ridge. It's not what you'd see in your movies or books. The devil exists, but he looks much more like a frozen Goliath than a scrawny red guy with horns and a pointed tail. It's best to know that should you run into Him.

Being on this train is all I can do now. It beats staying in Hell and walking around with ice in your eyes and on your tongue, even on your dick unless it falls off from the cold. That's horrible, but it's fixable.

Wanna come join me on the Nightmare Train?

Once I brought a man to his daughter's funeral five years in the future. He broke down, crying like a baby after someone took his favorite stuffed animal away. Pathetic bastard. Another time I brought a little girl to the pits of Hell where everyday she got to live her most embarrassing moment in school: peeing her pants in front of all her friends. I laughed each and every night.

How could I not?

But once I did prevent a school bus from crashing.

I kept giving a dad the same, recurring nightmare that his son's school bus was going to crash into a Mack truck and kill all but three students. It spooked him so much he lost it, followed the bus that day making big stink about everyone dying. The little kiddies were safe and he's spending time being evaluated in a psych hospital. But just as well—I did my part.

The old guy will never be the same. That's my job, and I've got to keep the engine rolling on this railway to Hell.

You shouldn't be too afraid until the end. I guess I should tell you that most of the time I scare people so much they end up taking their own lives; people have thrown themselves out windows, taken bottles worth of pills, forced themselves to drown in the tub, slit their wrists. Oh and one time—my personal favorite—a woman stuck her head in the oven. When the timer was done, so was she. Ah, memories. Nothing like a warming, heartfelt story to brighten up those gloomy days of your self-absorbed, pitiful life, right? But you wouldn't know what the hell I'm talking about. Things are just black and white to you. People all too often forget about the grey area, the area that blends the two worlds together, dark and light.

I don't judge either. They hop on my train or they don't. Most of the time they do. They're lost souls traveling through whatever strange galaxies I choose; reality is just a state of mind for the unaware, for the unconscious and for the oblivious of what's going on behind closed doors, beneath the shadows and around realism. I'm just a servant for those far greater in power than I, or you. I roll my way on through to the next person.

Joseph McGee

And it may be you.

There are intersections in our life that people wish not to contend with, that they wish never to relive; some of them so horrible that ordinary folks wouldn't think twice about suicide to stop it from happening again. People have murdered and gotten away freely, others have raped children or robbed grandmothers.

I left my old ways behind, and now I'm rebelling against forces that even scare the hell out of me.

One of my Lost Souls brought it up to me.

"Why do you commit such horrible acts?"

"Because it's my job," I replied.

"But do you like your job?"

I looked at the Lost Soul sort of funny, as if it could change my way of thinking with such simple words. I was being analyzed by someone that you could've said I kidnapped—and you'd be right. I did kidnap this one; I took all of them. This is my locomotive, with over a hundred confined souls stretched out to serve eternity running up and down the tracks while I incessantly ask for their ticket stubs. They must have their ticket stubs or they'll be thrown into the ice-waters of Leviathan, I tell them. And that's when their voices become a union of hissing and shrill moans.

My next stop: 1147 South 42nd Street.

Mr. Norman Bailey.

Mr. Bailey is a child molester, but the charges were dropped. The parents didn't want their nine-year-old daughter to go through the torture of telling her story a dozen times to a dozen different people, or so said *Times*—and yes, I do read the newspaper. It helps me keep track of who's been naughty or nice. I guess that makes me a kind of Santa Claus. I know when you're sleeping; I know when you're awake—so watch out for The Nightmare Train making a pit stop in the depths of your soul.

The sun was shining on the November morning. Snow had christened the ground the night before and had crystallized the trees and building with a glow of unique proportion. While little Samantha Clark was playing in her yard on East 42nd Street, Mr. Bailey muffled her with a scarf and dragged her along into his sedan, parked just a few feet away. She was prey to the monster at hand. He showed no pity.

Tonight there would be no mercy for him.

An angel of vengeance has certain rules to abide by. My rules are few and simple.

Cause as much disheartening pain as possible.

Make sure there's emotional distress.

127

Make them see the damage they've done and unleash pure terrorizing horror unto them.

Mr. Bailey slept alone tonight, the sheets wrapped around him firmly, keeping the winter chill at bay while he dreamed of children. And I hate that, to be honest. I think the guy's a lowlife.

Maybe mommy held him too close, or daddy never did.

Some call it a sickness, and they have groups, like AA meetings or Gamblers' Anonymous, but this wasn't an addiction to booze or gambling away your life savings at the craps table.

This went beyond self-indulged sickness.

In his mind, he was with that little girl again. He ran his memory in slow motion, reveling in every detail, enjoying it so much he began to get a little hot under the collar—and in his shorts.

I had to intervene.

I stopped his lustful dream and gave him something new to think about.

It would've been six hours before his alarm clock went off, waking him for another day of serving burgers and fries at the diner downtown. So before then, let me give him a nightmare cocktail.

Mr. Bailey was a fat man, but not just any kind of fat—the kind you see on *Jerry Springer* around Thanksgiving throwing turkey and mashed potatoes at each other. His head was bald and polished with a glossy glaze. It was a wonder he never had a heart attack from his dreams. A man of that size with an erection was something beyond scary. But it was kids he was attracted to, and that made him hell bound.

The room was dark and a little girl sat up on the bed in a thin lace nightgown. Her smile was seductive, her long blonde hair just covering her undeveloped breasts. As Mr. Bailey walked to her with his large belly sticking out, his face unshaved and a rotting odor permeating from him, she let him have it in the groin. A straight kick to the crotch, like a punter on an NFL team—straight up and away.

He rolled sideways, holding himself and landing on the bed, which squealed like a slaughtered pig under his massive pressure. Leather straps sprung from the darkness, wrapping his legs and arms up tight. A cloaked figure walked into the spattering of light that echoed from a single lamp on the scuffed night table and watched him.

Mr. Bailey was terrified, and had that not been one of my nightmare concoctions, I'd say he would've wet himself like he'd done until he was eleven. His beady eyes grew wide and bright; sweat dripped from his brow. Death was taking over.

The cloaked figure, now a silhouette in the shadows, reached out and tore down Mr. Bailey's pants, revealing his four-inch member, and with a slice of a meat cleaver, shortened it even more.

Blood spewed like Old Faithful. He cried out in pain. Maroon painted his blue button-down shirt, which seemed as if it were going to burst from the pressure of his enormous stomach. The figure took one more look at his testicles, dug into them with the edge of the blade and tore them off. They dropped to the ground a mix of blood and fluids. His evil was no more.

He was strapped to the bed, helpless, just like the little girl had been.

And every night for the next month, I made sure he had the same nightmare over and over again. That was always enough time to make a man go insane and realize he's nothing but dog shit on the shoe of society.

It only took eighteen days for Mr. Bailey to breakdown, confess to the police and render himself guilty in front of a jury of his peers, but that really made no difference to me. I'm nothing but a figment in someone's horrible imagination, like I am in yours.

It took nine days in prison for word to get around about what Mr. Bailey had done. It took an additional three days before he was murdered by a lifer with nothing to lose.

So this is what I do. This is what I'm good at.

And my next passenger is in Cleveland. A murder written off on a technicality, but we'll fix that, *won't we?*

I look at the passengers that travel with me on this running heap of punishment. With pleasure, they seem to look at me and wonder where I went wrong and where I went right.

Well, the truth is, to save my daughter from a lifetime of misfortune and regret, I need to stop a man in South Carolina before it's too late, and if I hurry with Mr. Daily in Cleveland, I'll have more than enough time to stop Mr. Donaldson from hurting my little girl. Even though I'm no longer around to see her, I'm still protecting my baby. I'll be damned if I'm going to let some murderous fiend hurt my Stephanie, torture her and kill her. I have twelve days to stop it. I almost feel bad for Mr. Donaldson when he messes with the conductor's precious little girl.

Mr. Bailey was nothing compared to the hurt I'll bring to Mr. Donaldson.

And I have a special seat for him.

Right. Next. To. Me.

The Reaper

AFTERWORD

I want to thank you. You as in the person reading this little inscription at the end of The Reaper. I wanted to sit down a while with you, talk to you, and explain for a moment about this story.

The Reaper was originally supposed to be strewn together with a previous publisher. It was supposed to be out, according to the release date listed on BN.com (Barnes & Noble) on March 31, 2008. Shit happens, right?

The reason The Reaper was shelved is, and probably forever will be, a mystery to me. That's fine. It has a new home with Snuff Books. I'm grateful for the heart and dedication this new publisher has put behind it; I'm proud to be its first publication in an ever-growing sea of books.

The Reaper has been expected for several months, and because of the internet hype built around it, it's coming out in a shorter time frame than a normal book would've been released.

This has been a long time coming.

I can go on and on about how this book should treat you well—I won't.

I could ask you, beg you to keep buying my books because I'm a new guy—I won't.

The truth of the matter is: You guys matter at the end of the day. I could sell a couple hundred or a couple hundred thousand copies, but it's not worth anything if everyone hated it, if it was worse than monkey shit on a warm day.

You, Continuous Reader—you're the reason why I do what I do; you're the heart and soul of this operation. Don't let anyone tell you differently. Writers could not be writers without your generous support

I hope you enjoy this tale I put together for you. And remember, I'm always available to be contacted one way or another.

You rock!

—Joseph McGee
July 2008
Worcester, MA

ABOUT THE AUTHOR

JOSEPH MCGEE is a published author. His novels include
In the Wake of the Night, *Snow Hill*, and
A Cold Day in Hell (coming soon).

He has dozens of short stories and articles that have appeared
in *Shroud Magazine*, *The Pulse Magazine* and *The Sound of Horror*
among others.

He is a Preditors & Editors award finalist.

Joe resides in Massachusetts with his four rescued felines
You can visit him at www.josephmcgee.net.

Breinigsville, PA USA
16 November 2010

249502BV00001B/4/P